D0242002

Other books by Babette Cole

Mummy Laid an Egg
Dr Dog
Drop Dead
Two of everything
Hair in Funny Places

ANIMALS

SCARE
ME
STIFF!

For Thomas

First published 2000
1 3 5 7 9 10 8 6 4 2
© Babette Cole 2000

Babette Cole has asserted her right under
the Copyright, Designs and Patents Act 1988
to be identified as the author of this work

First published in the United Kingdom in 2000 by
Jonathan Cape Limited, Random House
20 Vauxhall Bridge Road
London, SW1V 2SA

A CIP catalogue record of this book
is available at the British Library

ISBN 0224047078

Printed in Singapore

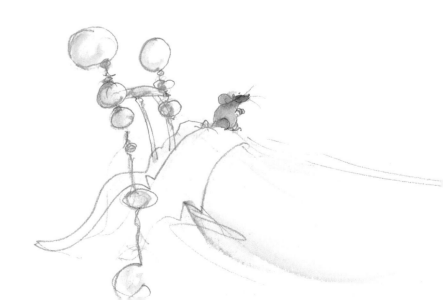

Babette Cole

ANIMALS SCARE ME STIFF

A Tom Maschler Book
JONATHAN CAPE
LONDON

Tom is followed by a dog.

He thinks,
It will eat me.

Then a horse joins in.

Now Tom is
frightened he will
be smashed
to pieces.

The bull tucks in behind.

oooh !

To the SEA !

He will toss me over a cliff,
thinks Tom.

A snake slithers up.
Tom feels sick.

They squeeze you to death,
snakes do!

And as for those
horrible birds...

They peck off your ears.

No, not spiders.

He just knew
they would
crawl up his
nose!

EEEK, BATS!

I bet one of them
is a vampire and
it will suck out
my blood.

The animals come right up and sniff Tom.

He is so frightened he
sinks to the ground
(he does not see the ants).

AAAgH!

Tom gives a terrible scream and tears off his trousers.

The
animals
fled in
terror.
It was
such a
horrible
sight.

They were now more
frightened of Tom than
he was of them.

Even the ants ran for cover…

Now he knows
what to do,
he's not scared
any more.

WWWWAAA'H!